The Agency Dick:

The case of Joy Lovejoy

by PuckDaddy

This is a true story.

It happened in a U.S. federal bureau called the National Guard.

I won't say which state it happened in, and I've changed names and "Salvadore Dali'd" people and places to protect the guilty. But it's true.

Seriously, I can't make this stuff up.

Email the author: **PuckDaddy@outlook.com**

The story contained herein is fiction, coming entirely from the voices inside the author's head. Any resemblance of this story's characters, narrative and dialogue to any living person is entirely coincidental and wholly unintentional- AFDW/PA Spartans included.

ISBN-13: 978-0692732632

Dedicated

to the

bureaucrats

operating the U.S. Government-

supervisors and non-supervisors, GS- and WG-, bargaining

and non-bargaining, teleworkers and cubicle-mongers,

METRO riders and traffic-jam drivers, management and

hourly workers and everyone else humping to keep the

government strong-

heroes all.

Thanks people.

Keep up the good work!

1.

Monday morning, still early, and Dimond Cooper sat at his office desk drinking coffee and surfing emails. He didn't notice the tall blonde from Finance standing in the doorway. He clicked on a page advertising HR's "Chili Cook-off" as the blonde stepped in front of his monitor and unbuttoned her blouse. A red blouse with yellow polka dots and big, blue buttons. The buttons popped like corks from a champagne bottle.

"Whoa!" Cooper said. His mother would've said the blonde was "full figured." His father would've said she was "stacked." All Dimond Cooper could say was, "Whoa!"

In fact, Cooper said "Whoa!" four or five times as the woman's lily-white breasts poured over a satiny black bra. She pulled out both sides of the polka dot blouse like an angel spreading her wings.

"Do I need to unhook my bra too?"

"Whoa!" Cooper said again. He scooted back from his desk and coffee splashed from his cup, the white one with the gold "Army" logo he'd swiped from the recruiters.

"Can you see my complaint?" the blonde said. "Or do I need to unhook my bra too?"

"I'm sorry lady," Cooper said. "You must, uh, you must have the wrong office."

"I didn't mean to startle you." She let the blouse fall to the sides of her large breasts and yanked some tissues from the box on his desk. "You've spilled your coffee. Let me help."

"No! Oh no, really. It's no problem," Cooper said. "You didn't startle me. You scared the shit out of me."

The woman laughed and her laugh was nearly as unexpected as her display of flesh- throaty and deep.

"Really," she said. "I didn't mean to startle you. I just wanted to get here early and show you my complaint before the rest of HR arrives."

"Uh-huh."

Now she crossed her arms like a shelf to rest the heavy breasts. "Aren't you Dimond Cooper?"

"Coop."

"Excuse me?"

"I'm Coop. Been Coop since the first grade. Who are you?"

"I'm Joy Lovejoy. I work in Finance."

"Good morning Ms. Lovejoy."

"Good morning. I am sorry about making you spill your coffee."

"That's okay. One of the hazards of being a bureaucrat."

"And it splashed all over your pretty tie."

"Yeah, I didn't see that. Oh well, I get a new one every Father's Day. Listen, can I help you with something? Standing in my office with your shirt off doesn't look good."

"It doesn't look good?"

"Well, I mean, yeah, it looks good…to me. You look good to me. But it probably won't look good to someone walking through the hallway."

"Want me to close the door?"

"No! No, I just want you to, to, you know, button up your shirt."

"OK, but I want you to see my complaint. You are the guy who runs the agency's complaint department, right?"

"Complaint department? Yeah, I guess you could say that. I'm actually the Labor guy. I administer the labor contracts between the unions and TAG."

"TAG? You mean The Adjutant General?"

"Yes. The Adjutant General. You know, the two-star general who runs this agency?"

"Right. But you investigate complaints?"

"You mean grievances. Yes, sometimes. But mostly I just make sure grievances are formatted properly and delivered to the correct supervisor. Do you have a grievance?"

"Yes. I'm showing it to you." Joy Lovejoy pulled out the sides of the red blouse again, spreading her wings wide. "My boobs are too big."

3

2.

Dimond Cooper
Monday, 7 March
Memorandum For Record (MFR)

//UNCLASS//

Lots of good Americans work for the federal government (last I heard it was more than four million). And about 50,000 of these federal workers are fulltime Guardsmen known as "Dual-Status Technicians"- they wear military uniforms and drill one weekend a month at the local armory or air base to keep their jobs.

I'm one of these fulltime Technicians, but I don't wear a military uniform or drill on the weekend because I'm a classified as a "Non-Dual Status Technician."

Confusing? Hey, it's the government. What do you expect? Anyway, if you're reading this MFR, chances are you work for a branch of the U.S. government, probably a Congressman's office or the Inspector General, and more than likely you're investigating the Joy Lovejoy case.

Well, OK then, let me lay it out for you in easy-to-read fashion:

Ms. Joy Lovejoy, a Non-Dual Status Technician who works in Finance here at Joint Forces Headquarters, visited my office this morning. Ms. Lovejoy is blonde and kind of tall. And built. Definitely built. Very curvy in all the curvy places.

4

And as it turns out, the curves are responsible for her visit. Seems Ms. Lovejoy's supervisor, Colonel Roy Lester, makes constant references to her breasts and she wants to file a grievance to make him stop. Maybe. First she wants to explore her options.

Full disclosure: Ms. Lovejoy showed me her breasts during this morning's meeting. I did not, repeat: DID NOT, in any way, prompt or encourage this action. She flashed me to prove she possesses two major causes for grievance.

I'm a married man and felt duty-bound to inform her that I'm not an expert in mammalian protuberances, as I've only viewed my wife's breasts during the last 20 years (though I would confess under questioning that Ms. Lovejoy's causes for grievance are large, appear firm and seem to defy gravity). After witnessing this "unveiling," I believe she's telling the truth and that her pronounced physical accouterments attract unwanted attention from her supervisor.

And for the record, and in case my wife should ever get a copy of this MFR (Love you Honey ☺), I only briefly eyed the evidence before beating a hasty retreat for a fresh cup of coffee.

When I returned to my office, I asked Ms. Lovejoy if she'd rather file an Equal Opportunity (EO) complaint since the regs prohibit filing a grievance and an EO complaint on the same matter.

Ms. Lovejoy hesitated and said she doesn't want to get COL Lester in trouble and that she actually feels sorry for him. She said he stares at her naturals and then loses his concentration and starts to babble. She said it wasn't his fault that "my boobies are so tittilating." (Her words, not mine.)

I informed Ms. Lovejoy the timeline for filing a grievance expires 15 days after the cause occurs, and I explained that a properly formatted grievance must- 1. Explain the problem, and; 2. Explain how the problem should be fixed.

In the end, Ms. Joy Lovejoy refused to file an official grievance. She said she might change her mind and file a grievance within the next 15 days if COL Lester doesn't change his ways and stop "eyeballing my boobies and drooling like a 2-year-old." (Again, her words- not mine.)

I can't make this stuff up.

//UNCLASS//

3.

"Coop!" The man yelling from the conference room was muscled and bald. A scowl stamped his face and he looked like a middle linebacker for a pro football team. His name was Jerome Robinson and he had, in fact, once tried out for a pro football team after his college days at West Point ended. He'd been a young lieutenant then. Now he was an old colonel.

"Coop!" Robinson yelled again.

"Yes sir." Dimond Cooper strolled into the conference room already packed with attendees. He carried a clipboard in one hand and steaming cup of coffee in the other. "Right here Boss."

"My meetings start at 0900." Robinson raised his wrist and tapped his watch with a short, stubby finger.

"Yes sir, I'm fully cognizant of your meetings' mandated start time."

"It's now 0905."

"Thank you sir."

"I am this agency's Human Resource Officer, Coop."

"Yes sir, you are."

"And you are this agency's Labor Relations Specialist."

"Yes sir, I am."

"I am wearing the battle dress uniform of a soldier ready for battle."

"Yes sir, you are."

"And you are wearing a blue blazer and a faggoty-looking yellow tie with a, a, what is that? A coffee stain?"

"Yes sir, I am. And yes sir, it is." Cooper ducked his head and spoke in a loud whisper: "But I'd say calling it 'faggoty' is a little, you know, not cool."

"Not cool?" Robinson's scowl disappeared and he coughed a little to clear his throat. "No. I guess that's not cool. I used the wrong word."

"Should've said 'sissy' tie," SGM Chesterson said.

"Right you are, Chet," Robinson said. "But I will say I'm still the boss. A freakin' colonel in the United States Army can say that. Can't I say that, Coop?"

"Yes sir. You can say that."

"And I will say timing wins the battle."

Cooper nodded. "Timing. Yes sir."

"Timing."

"Timing."

An hour and 12 minutes later, Colonel Robinson's weekly Monday morning meeting finally finished. It'd been a routine Monday morning meeting with no big surprises, especially if you didn't count the swear word that slipped from the chaplain's lips when he was debriefing last Saturday's "Youth Day" at the downtown armory.

And now that the meeting was over, Cooper sat patiently at the conference table, not bothering to bum rush the door like the rest of the attendees. "Colonel Robinson," he said. "Can I get a minute?"

"Is it important?"

"Yes sir. This is something for your ears only."

A crew of confidantes stuck to the colonel like rock-star groupies. They heard the word "important" and stopped shoving toward the exit.

Robinson poked his thumb in their direction. "These guys can't hear?"

"No sir, this needs to be kept completely confidential."

"Alright. But if this is about one of my peeps here, then I think they got a right to hear about it before I fire them!"

"OK sir. I thought you wanted to fire them all at once, so…" Cooper shrugged.

Robinson chuckled and shooed the groupies out the door. "You guys need to leave. The Labor guru here has some secret stuff to share. And no, we're not firing you guys. Are we Coop?" He chuckled again. "Close that door, Murphy."

Cooper waited until the room cleared and the door shut. "OK Boss," he said. "Ready for this?"

"Shoot."

"Had a lady come into my office this morning asking about how to file a grievance."

"Is that why you were late to my meeting? You know, Coop, I was only kiddin' about that timing thing."

"Yes sir. I understand. Keeping up appearances."

"Yeah. That's right."

"Well, this grievance has everything to do with appearances."

"Is it about me? What? She doesn't like my face?" Robinson smiled big and his white teeth sparkled.

"No sir, nothing to do with you. This one concerns another colonel."

"Really?"

"Yes sir. And since the grievance wasn't filed, I'm not really at liberty to name names. But, you know, since it's centered on an O-6 and the agency has been taking shots from the newspaper lately-"

"Dammit!" The linebacker's scowl flashed red. "Is this about Colonel Lester?"

"Again sir. I shouldn't name names."

"Is it Colonel Lester?"

"Yes."

"Shit! I knew it. That freakin' idiot is gonna get us all back on the front page of the Star. What'd he do this time?"

"Sir, seems the good colonel can't keep his mouth shut around a certain Non-Dual Status female Technician."

"Lovejoy?"

"Sir, I shouldn't say."

"Is it Joy Lovejoy from Finance?"

"Yes."

"Shit! I knew it. That freakin' pervert! What's he doin'? Tellin' sex stories about his time back in college?"

"I haven't heard that sir. What Ms. Lovejoy is alleging is that he can't stop talking about her breasts. And it's making her uncomfortable."

"That freakin' idiot!" Robinson glanced around the empty room and leaned toward Cooper: "Have you seen her tits?"

"Uh. Yes sir. I've seen them."

"Wow huh?"

"Yes sir."

Robinson sat back and let the rage return. "That pervert! That freakin' idiot has got to wise up! An O-6 can't go around a female Technician talking about her breasts nowadays. This isn't 1997 for god sakes!"

"Yes sir."

"Is she gonna file a grievance or an EO complaint?"

"Sir, right now she says neither. She just wants the good colonel to keep his mouth shut. Doesn't want me to talk to anyone about this either. Not yet anyway. Said she won't file anything if it stops."

"Shit! I knew it. That freakin' colonel is gonna get us all fired. I'll talk to him."

"Yes? Well you'll have to use some tact, sir. We can't let him tell Lovejoy that he knows she came to us. That'll be retaliation and-"

"We'll have to fire that freakin' nut if he retaliates."

11

"Yes sir."

"Shit! I knew it. That guy is out of control. Out. Of. Con. Trol."

A knock sounded on the conference room door and one of Robinson's minions poked his head in.

"Colonel, I have to interrupt," the minion said. "You've got that meeting with TAG."

"Yeah, yeah. Listen Dimond. I'll talk to the good colonel. Don't worry. He won't retaliate."

"OK, Boss. Just want to protect you and keep this thing in-house. We don't need a Congressman's office, or some Inspector General from National Guard Bureau nosing around. We sure don't need to be front-page news again."

"You are right." Robinson stood up and headed for the door but stopped behind Cooper's ear and whispered: "What about the Cockran thing?"

"The Cockran thing?"

"Yeah, you know, that thing at the Air Guard Base."

"Oh. Yes sir. I'm working it, sir," Cooper said. "Working it."

"OK. Keep me updated."

"Yes sir."

Robinson headed toward the door again. "Shit!" he said. "I knew it. That freakin' guy's gonna get us all fired! Get on this Coop."

"Yes sir."

4.

Dimond Cooper
Monday, 7 March
Memorandum For Record (MFR)

//UNCLASS//

MFR #2 for 7 March: Quite a Monday this is shaping up
to be. First, Joy Lovejoy and her lovelies. And now, the
Cockran thing. Barely lunchtime and I'm already writing a
second Memorandum for Record. So, for the record- Colonel
Robinson has asked me to look into the handling of the
Cockran affair and make a recommendation. I'm heading to
the Air Guard Base in the morning. I'll nose around Command
there and see what they say about why Senior Master Sergeant
Jaxston Cockran was denied re-enlistment.

Of course, being denied re-enlistment is a military decision,
not something HR on the Technician side should be looking
into. But I'm going to investigate the matter because COL
Robinson thinks there might be some spillover.

Don't know what that spillover might be yet. But I'm a
bureaucrat and I have my orders. Tomorrow I'm off on a
mission that summons my extra-ordinary bureaucratic skills:
Faster than a speeding PowerPoint slide, more powerful than a
loco colonel, able to leap tall BS in a single bound- It's
SuperLaborDude! Wow. I know. Right?
//UNCLASS//

5.

"Good morning," the gate guard said. "License please."

"License?" Cooper had just rolled up to the gatehouse at the Air Guard Base, on the other side of the airport. His window was down and he held out his CAC card. "How about my government I.D. card?"

"Excuse me?" The civilian guard took off his hat and put his hand to his ear. He was an older man and his OD green uniform looked like it fell off the "Vietnam" rack at the back of the Army-Navy surplus store. Or it could've come from the pile of uniforms he'd stashed in his closet after retirement back in the day.

"My government I.D. card," Cooper said. "You know, my CAC card? Here's mine."

"What?"

"I said-" Cooper shut his mouth and flipped open his wallet. He slid his driver's license free and handed it to the guard.

"Gets busy here some days," the guard said. "Oughta have your license out and ready so's you don't hold up the line."

"No doubt."

"No, you don't have to get out. Your license is good enough."

"I'm looking for Colonel Hart," Cooper said. "The Wing Commander."

"The Wing Commander is Colonel Hart."

"Right."

"That's right."

"Is his office in the hangar? Or in the Wing Building?"

"Colonel Hart. Yes, that's right. Have a good day." The guard turned and shuffled back to the gatehouse.

"You too!" Cooper replaced his license and eased the car onto the base.

The old man waved. "Have your license out and ready next time!"

"Yes sir. We'll do."

Cooper parked behind the Wing Building and wandered its hallways until he found the suite with "Commander" painted on its glass entry doors.

An Airman 1st Class sat behind the glass doors at a desk blocking the entrance to Colonel Hart's office. She wore Air Force blues- a skirt, a short sleeve shirt and a colorful rack of ribbons- and her black hair was pinned in a tight bun. Pearl earrings swelled from her tiny lobes.

Cooper was impressed and approached the big desk like a defendant in court. "Colonel Hart please?"

"He's still in the Commander's morning meeting," the A1C said. She wore a nametag stamped THURSTON. "Are you Mr. Cooper?"

"I'm Coop. Been Coop since the first grade." He reached out and shook her hand. "Pleased to meet you. How'd you know who I am?"

"Colonel Hart said to be on the lookout for an old guy wearing a tie."

"Oh. Yeah. Well, I guess I qualify. Old white dude in civvies. But I'm really not that old."

"So, he wasn't trying to be, you know, mean or anything. He just wanted me to know what you look like 'cause he wants to know as soon as you get here."

"I see. But I didn't tell anyone I was coming. How'd he know I'd be here today?"

"Don't know."

"Are you new here, A1C Thurston?"

"This is my third week. How'd you know that?"

"I saw your name on a list of new hires at Joint Forces Headquarters. I work there and we in-process all new Technicians for the state."

"Oh." Her head bent forward, examining her cell phone. It rang and she spun around in her chair to whisper the conversation.

"OK then," Cooper said. He drifted around the room looking at airplane pictures hanging on the walls, waiting for A1C Thurston's call to end. That's when the glass doors opened and an excited voice called out.

"Coop!"

16

"Major Newman!" Cooper said. "The legend! What's happening man?"

"I'm good, I'm good. What are you doing here?"

"The government's business my good fellow. Just trying to support the troops and keep freedom's fires burning. You know me."

"Yeah, I know you!"

The two men traded handshakes and manly half-hugs and Newman lowered his voice: "You got a minute?"

"Think so. Just trying to get in to see Colonel Hart."

"Real quick. Step out in the hall with me. I gotta tell you something."

Out in the hall, Newman wasted no time: "Coop, I know why you're here. It's the Cockran thing, right?"

"Uh, yeah, well. You know."

"Is it an official investigation? I need to tell you something but I can't be put under oath."

"Major. Come on. You know how this works. Everything's preliminary right now. If I determine a full-blown inquiry is warranted, then HRO will tap an officer to conduct an official 15-6 investigation."

"That's what I thought. I heard you were coming up here to check on this."

"Who told you?"

"My spies."

"Yeah? Well you must have an extensive network 'cause I didn't tell anyone I was coming, not even Colonel Hart."

"I know things." Newman tapped his temple. "And about this Cockran fubar I know lots of things."

"Tell me."

A1C Thurston pecked on the glass doors and motioned. "Colonel Hart is ready for you," she mouthed.

Newman elbowed Cooper. "I guess I'm not the only one who knew you were coming. Come talk to me after you get finished, Coop. I'll tell you the rest of the story."

6.

Dimond Cooper
Tuesday, 8 March
Memorandum For Record (MFR)

//UNCLASS//

I'm in Col. Hart's office right now, and since Colonel Hart is an Air Force officer I'll follow Air Force customs and abbreviate "Colonel" as "Col."

At this very moment he's speaking to me and I'm writing this MFR on a memo pad like I'm back in college taking notes of the endless dribble flowing from the pie hole of a pompous professor. Only this professor doesn't have the smudged, half-erased green chalkboard crossing the room behind him. Instead, a picture window behind his desk overlooks a line of A-10 'Warthog' aircraft, those tank killers the Army grunts love. Of course, Col. Hart is as pompous as any professor I remember, but the view over his shoulder is much better.

OK. Well, he's not telling me anything. Says the decision not to reenlist Senior Master Sergeant Jaxston Cockran was made by the commander based on manning. Uh-huh. The Wing is below 97 percent manned. But whatever. I suppose he is right about reenlistment being a military decision made by the commander, not something a Technician like me has any right asking about.

For crying out loud, this guy's a jerk. He just told me to communicate to COL Robinson that the Air Guard operates a little differently than the Army Guard. "I know Colonel Robinson is a big man in the Army," Hart just said. "But I'm the biggest man on this base. So you tell him to stay out of my business."

Yes sir.

"And you're nothing but a technocrat."

He just called me a technocrat? What the hell is a technocrat? I'd ask but I'm too busy scrambling down these notes to open my mouth.

"This is the Air Guard," he said. "Go back to that puzzle palace at Joint Forces Headquarters and stay out of our business."

OK. Enough of this. Got it. This technocrat is out of here.

//UNCLASS//

7.

Major Newman wasn't waiting outside the glass doors when Cooper left the Commander's Office. So it surprised Cooper when Newman appeared in the hallway walking right beside him.

"Coop! So what did the Big Guy say?"

"Jeez, Newman. Where'd you come from?"

"What did the Big Guy say?"

"He said, he said a bunch of stuff. I'm looking into this situation in an official unofficial capacity. You understand."

"Yes?"

"Well. I just can't tell you everything that was said."

"He didn't say shit."

"I was in there for more than half an hour."

"He didn't say shit, did he. Did he?"

"No. Not really."

"Let's step in the break room. I'll tell you what you need to know."

"OK. I need a fresh cup of coffee anyway."

"Man, you still drinking coffee night and day? I swear, if I ever need blood I want it from you. There's enough caffeinated energy in your veins to fuel an A-10."

In the break room, Newman bought a candy bar from the snack machine and started talking. "Listen," he said. "I was in the room when the decision was made not to reenlist Cockran."

"Yeah?"

"And I don't care what Colonel Hart says, it's got nothing to do with manning."

Cooper poured the last drop of coffee from the break room's stained pot. It was cold and bitter and, like all military coffee, black enough to blot out the sun.

"Tell me about it," Cooper said.

"This is totally off-the-record."

"OK. I might need to use it anonymously."

"Not with my name."

"Is your name Anonymous?"

"Seriously. I could get my ass fired for this."

"C'mon. You know me. Wild horses couldn't get me to talk. I know how to keep secrets."

"Yeah right. You give up easier than a bride on her wedding night."

"You haven't met my wife. I thought she'd be a virgin 'til her second marriage."

"I'm serious, Coop."

"OK, I can see you don't trust me. But if a Technician gets fired in this state I'm the guy doing the paperwork and sweating the details. So listen, they can't fire you for telling the truth."

"No, but they can non-retain me on the military side- just like they're doing to Cockran right now. Then I lose my fulltime job automatically."

"You're a federal Technician. You get 30 days to work after you lose military membership. But I get your point."

"So don't give out my name?"

Cooper snapped to attention and saluted: "You have my word as an honorably retired airman."

"OK man, I'm trusting you. Here it is: Senior Master Sergeant Cockran got raped."

"What?"

"Yeah dude. Pants down. Full penetration."

"Raped?"

"Yeah dude. It was brutal."

"You gotta be shittin' me."

"Dude. Jaxston Cockran got raped. By another airman."

8.

Dimond Cooper
Wednesday, 9 March
Memorandum For Record (MFR)

//FOR OFFICIAL AUTHORIZATION ONLY//

This memorandum for record is my testimony to what was said during my visit to the Air Guard Base on Tuesday, 8 March. Specifically, this memo details what was said by an officer at the Wing familiar with circumstances surrounding the denial of reenlistment to Senior Master Sergeant Jaxston Cockran.

The officer referenced above said Cockran reported to have been raped by a fellow airman. He said Cockran filed a "Restricted" report of the attack with the Wing's Equal Opportunity (EO) Manager. Of course, this "Restricted" report cannot be made public without Cockran's approval. Cockran can use the report to gain access to some medical and psychological help, and to gather evidence in case he decides to press charges at a later date.

Anyway, the officer said the Wing Commander, Col. Hart, learned about the "Restricted" report and ordered Cockran's commander, Lt. Col. Leslie Collins, to deny Cockran's reenlistment.

Apparently, according to the officer who related all this to me in confidence, Col. Hart doesn't think SMS Cockran should have reported the rape. The officer said he was in the room when the order to deny Cockran's reenlistment was made, and he heard Hart say: "He probably enjoyed it. The fucker should've fought back," and "I don't want no pussies in this Wing."

Wow.

Now what is my next move? Everything I heard is in confidence. It's also second hand. I trust the officer who confided in me, but I can't use his words to help Cockran. Don't think I can do anything to help Cockran, not officially anyway. I can't even tell him I know what happened to him. Really don't know what I can do because denying reenlistment is a military decision. The commander has all the power to make whatever decision is best for his unit.

But...hell. Gotta do something. I can't let Cockran get raped twice.

//FOR OFFICIAL AUTHORIZATION ONLY//

9.

"Coop!"

Colonel Jerome Robinson bellowed through the maze of offices.

"Coop!"

Cooper was on the phone. He made apologies and hung up hastily, but not before Robinson's scowling mug plugged up his office doorway.

"Coop!"

"Yes sir. I was just on the phone."

"Didn't you hear me calling for you?"

"Yes sir. I was on the phone."

"Listening to a grievance?"

"Well, sir, I have to-"

Robinson didn't wait for the answer. He walked in and dropped his large frame in the chair facing Cooper's desk. Then he belched, tapping his chest with his fist like a judge opening court.

"How'd yesterday's visit to the Air Base go? You get to talk to Colonel Hart?"

"Yes sir," Cooper said.

"He tell you something good?"

"No sir. Not one good thing. Nothing's good at the Air Guard Base. It's ugly."

"I was afraid of that. Who was on the phone?"

26

"Just now?"

"Was it Lovejoy?" Robinson asked.

"Sir, I really shouldn't say."

"Joy Lovejoy from Finance?"

"Yes sir."

"God. What's she want?"

"Well sir, I have to say-"

"Has she decided to file a grievance?"

"Not yet, sir. I think she's still weighing her options."

Robinson's scowl twisted into a question mark. "What options? She can't stretch this thing out forever."

"No sir."

"I mean, she's only got a couple weeks to decide. Right? I mean, 15 days or something. Right?"

"That's right."

"God. So I spoke to Colonel Lester, that freakin' nut. He says he doesn't look at her, her, you know, her breasteses, but he says she's always showing them to him."

"She's showing them?"

"Yeah, he says she wears tight dresses on purpose. Says she wants him to look."

"Sir, really. That's bullshit. The lady has big breasts. OK. She can't hide them under a gunnysack. What's she supposed to do with them?"

"I know. I know, I told him that was bullshit. He says he might have to reassign her. Put her in another office."

"Not good."

"What?"

"Sir, that would be a very bad move for the agency."

"Why? He could just move her and take away the temptation. It's not like it's gonna cost her any money or anything."

"Sir. She didn't do anything wrong. We can't punish her for having big breasts."

"Have you seen them, Coop? I mean, of course you've seen them. Nice aren't they?"

"Yes sir, I've seen them."

"Really nice, huh?"

"Centerfold material. And maybe there is something to what Colonel Lester's saying, about how she wants him to look. But hey, she's got a right to be proud of her body. She shouldn't have to wrap herself up like one of those women you see walking behind a rag-headed terrorist."

Robinson rubbed a hand over his bald head and gaveled his chest to announce another belch.

"Sir, here's the thing," Cooper said. "We can't move her without a real cause. Otherwise we're changing a condition of employment."

"She's not in the union."

"Doesn't matter. She's a federal Technician and could file a grievance. Besides that, Colonel, if we move her now it could be construed as retaliation."

28

"Oh no. We don't want none of that retaliation shit. I remember old Colonel Shorter got accused of that, back when I was a captain? Hell, they retired him within the month. Bang. Gone."

Robinson stood up and closed the office door. When he turned around his face was dark and sober. "OK. No shit. What'd you find out about the Cockran thing?"

Cooper shook his head. "Seriously ugly."

"How do we make it go away?"

"Don't think we can. I think this one stays."

"What?"

"Somebody's going down for this one."

Robinson's eyelids drooped and his voice lowered. "Colonel Hart told me he had this thing under control."

"Colonel Hart is heading a conspiracy, sir. We can't back him on this one."

"Conspiracy? Careful Coop. You're talking about an O-6 here. Guy's a Wing Commander for god sakes."

"Colonel, I'm warning you to be careful. With all due respect. You know I've never let you down and I'm clanging an unofficial warning bell here: Colonel Hart is taking the wrong path on this one."

Robinson rubbed his head. "Coop, you know I trust you. But sometimes, well listen, this ain't the movies we're talkin' about here. Colonel Hart is not a bad guy. He's not the evil Dr. Nefarious out to destroy poor, innocent Sergeant Goody."

29

"Yes sir. I understand. This is real life. Good and evil isn't personified in the flesh. But in real life, people- even good people- do bad things."

Robinson's face flushed but he said nothing.

"Sir, tomorrow I'm going back to the Air Guard Base to interview Jaxston Cockran. I'll try to get his version of what's happening."

"Uh huh."

"But at this point I believe somebody's not telling the truth."

"Uh huh."

"And at this point I believe that someone is Colonel Hart."

"Uh huh."

"Sir, somebody's going down for this one."

Robinson pounded his chest and belched a dismissal. "OK Coop. Just remember what I said, this ain't the movies."

10.

"Good morning," the gate guard said. "Identification please."

Cooper's second visit to the Air Guard Base in three days prepared him to face the civilian gate guard decked out in the Vietnam–era uniform.

"Good morning," Cooper said. "Here's my license."

"Excuse me?" The guard leaned close to the car's open window.

"Here you go," Cooper said. "My license."

"Yes. That's your license."

"You want to see it?"

"I want to see what?"

"My license. Here it is. I need to get onto the base."

"I need to see your I.D. to let you onto the base. Got one?"

"You mean my CAC card?"

"CAC card."

Cooper flipped open his wallet and slid his CAC card free. He handed it to the guard. "You wanted my driver's license the other day, not my CAC card."

"Sir, I need to see your CAC card before entry. I don't make the rules 'round here, just doin' my job to make sure they're followed."

"Yes sir."

"Gets busy here some days," the guard said. "Oughta have your CAC card out and ready so's you don't hold up the line."

"I'll be sure to do that next time."

"No, it's alright. You don't have to pull over this time." The old guard removed his hat and cupped his ear. "Is that what you're asking?"

"No. It's good. Everything's fine."

"Yeah? Good, good. Colonel Hart's hard to find. Think he works in the Wing Building."

"Thanks."

"Yep." The guard shuffled back to the gatehouse. "Have a good day."

"You too!"

Cooper parked behind the Wing Building in the same spot he used on his last visit. His problem now was trying to figure out where Senior Master Sergeant Jaxston Cockran worked. He could trek up to the Commander's Office and ask A1C Thurston for help locating Cockran, but then she'd report his visit to Colonel Hart. No, he needed to fly under the radar on this one.

As he considered the situation, a Chief Master Sergeant stepped out the back of the building and lit a cigarette.

"Hey Chief," Cooper said as walked up to the man now inhaling the smoke.

"Hey."

"What's up?"

"Sneaking a cancer stick," the Chief said. "What's up with you?"

"I'm good. I'm looking for Senior Master Sergeant Cockran. You know him?"

"Jax? He works in AGE."

A single row of railroad tracks split this Air Guard Base east and west. Administrative support airmen work on the base's east side, and maintenance/operations airmen work on the base's west side. Cooper figured the AGE shop must be on the west side, close to the flight line.

"Across the tracks?"

"First building on the right," the Chief said. "Soon as you cross the tracks."

"Thanks Chief."

"Why do you want him?"

"What?" Cooper had already turned, was already walking back to his car when the Chief's question rang out.

"Why do you want him?"

Cooper hesitated. "Oh, just a, just need to talk to him a minute."

"He's not in a position to talk to anybody. Especially someone nosing around from Headquarters."

"Excuse me?"

"Aren't you from Headquarters? Used to work here years ago, didn't you?"

"Yes."

"Back then you wore a uniform."

"I retired militarily. Now I'm a Non-Dual Status Technician."

"Then you should know this is none of State HQ's business." The Chief took another drag of the cigarette. "We'll handle it."

"What are you talking about?"

"You know what I'm talking about." He flipped the cigarette to the ground and twisted his boot on it, moving deliberately and staring at Cooper like a schoolyard bully. Then he turned and disappeared back into the building.

AGE, which stands for Aerospace Ground Equipment, is the shop responsible for supplying and maintaining the equipment used by military aircraft preparing for flight. Five or six fulltime Guard Technicians work in the AGE shop, but they were all on the flight line when Cooper ambled in looking for SMS Cockran.

Cooper found a seat at the shop's break table and picked-up scattered euchre cards, shuffling the discarded 2s to 8s back into the pack for a round of solitaire. He played three rounds before the first A-10 airplane started up. It took four more solitaire rounds before he heard the planes roll to the runway for last chance check and, finally, take-off. He moved to the window and watched the Warthogs rumble down the runway

34

and up into the sky. Slow airplanes. Slow, loud airplanes. And ugly. Reminded Cooper of flying tanks.

"Hi there. Can I help you?" The voice rang from the shop entrance and trailed the speaker inside.

"I'm here to see Senior Master Sergeant Cockran," Cooper said. "Is he in today?"

"Who are you?"

Cooper stood and separated the cards back to a proper euchre deck. "I'm Coop. From the Human Resources Office at Joint Forces Headquarters."

Three more military technicians entered the shop, nodding to Cooper and moving about their business.

"Cockran's out on the line. Should be back here shortly."

"Thanks."

One of the technicians, a Technical Sergeant wearing an overcoat that covered his nametag, asked: "Aren't you the union guy?"

"I'm Coop. The state's Labor rep."

"Don't you deal with the union here?"

"Yes. I negotiate with your union. You guys all bargaining unit members?"

The Technicians exchanged glances. "Uh, we weren't invited."

"Invited?"

"We don't pay their dues so those union bastards won't let us go to their meetings."

35

"I see. But you're still covered by the union contract. They have to represent you whether you pay dues or not."

The Technicians didn't believe him.

"Seriously," Cooper said. "The law says if you're eligible to be in the bargaining unit, then the union must represent you."

"Even if we refuse to pay their dues?"

"Yes. Even then."

"Doesn't make much sense. If they have to represent us for free, then we'll never pay their dues."

"Like your gate guard here says, I don't make the rules boys, I only make sure they're followed."

The door to the AGE shop squeaked open and everyone turned to watch SMS Cockran walk in. He was tall and thin with bony arms jammed deep in his pockets. He spotted Cooper and turned and exited the building without a word.

Cooper looked at the Technicians. "That was Cockran, right?"

"Yes sir."

"Huh. Must be my face. I get that sometimes."

The Technical Sergeant in the overcoat shook his head. "No sir. Jax is going through a tough time right now. He's-"

"Things are just tough for him nowadays," said one of the other Technicians. "Jax probably doesn't want to talk to anybody right now."

"I guess not," Cooper said. "Alright, well, he doesn't have to talk to me. I'm just here to help. I know he's been non-retained by his commander and he's probably feeling bad about that."

"Yeah. Probably."

"Has he mentioned what he's gonna do after he gets kicked out? Where he's gonna work? Is he married?"

"Married with three kids. And his oldest daughter, still in high school? I guess she's knocked up. Tough times at the old Cockran house."

"Yeah, no kiddin'." Cooper pulled a business card from his wallet. "Give this to him when he gets back. And tell him to call me any time. I'm on his side."

"OK, but it won't do any good."

"Why?"

"Because the commander is bootin' him out. Technicians can't fight what the commander does."

"You'd be surprised. This is America. Anything can happen. Tell him to call me."

"The union said they couldn't help him."

"The union says a lot of things. Tell him to call me."

11.

Dimond Cooper
Friday, 11 March
Memorandum For Record (MFR)

//UNCLASS//

I'm writing this MFR from my office here at Joint Forces Headquarters. It's early in the morning and I want to get my thoughts on paper before the rest of HR shows up.

I visited the Air Guard Base yesterday to speak to Senior Master Sergeant Jaxston Cockran. I wanted to ask him why he thought he's being denied the opportunity to re-enlist. I didn't get a warm reception at the base- a Chief told me to mind my own business- and I never did get to talk to Cockran. He saw me and actually turned away. No doubt in my mind he knows I'm from HQ and he's afraid to talk to me. That man is going through some serious stress right now. A real shit storm. I must help him. Being a good Wingman means never leaving an airman behind, even if the airman is hurt and confused. Especially if the airman is hurt and confused.

Hold on Cockran. I'll help you.

//UNCLASS//

12.

"Good morning, Mr. Cooper."

"Oh, hello. Good morning."

"Did you get a chance to review my letter?" The man talking was a Technician from down the hall, a first-line supervisor wearing Army stripes on his uniform that identified him as a Sergeant First Class.

"Your letter?" Cooper, sitting at his desk and just finishing up the MFR, was slow to switch focus.

"Yes sir. You were gonna edit my Letter of Reprimand? The one I want to give to my soldier for sleeping at his desk?"

"Come on in," Cooper said. He took a drink of coffee and waved to the chair opposite his desk. "Have a seat. And by the way, I'm Coop. Been Coop since the first grade."

"Yes sir, I remember you saying that. Sir, I don't want to take your time. Just thought I'd check on that letter."

"When did you send it to me?" Cooper began scrolling emails to find something sent by the Sergeant First Class.

"No. I didn't email it to you. I dropped it off last week. Remember? You said you'd take a red pen to it and then I could correct it."

"Oh yes. I'll tell you Sergeant, it's been a hectic week. I apologize for not getting that letter back to you already." Cooper sorted through the papers on his desk. "Wonder where I put it? It's not popping out at me here."

"Can I bring you another copy? Maybe send it to you electronically?"

"I'd prefer that, actually."

"OK, no problem. That's what I'll do."

"Cool. Send it to me and I'll get it right back."

"OK. We'll do."

"Coop!"

The Sergeant First Class cocked his head toward Colonel Robinson's howl and decided to beat feet, stumbling over himself and getting out of the office just moments before the colonel's frame filled the doorway.

"Coop!"

"Yes sir."

"Oh, you're here today after all," Robinson said. He sagged against the doorframe and checked his watch. "I've got a meeting with the Old Man in about two minutes. Tell me what happened."

"You mean at the Air Guard Base yesterday?"

"Yeah. What'd Cockran say?"

"Boss, he saw me waiting for him and turned and walked the other way."

"You're shittin' me."

"No sir. He obviously didn't want to talk. His fellow workers say he's going through a hard time lately. Been kinda withdrawn."

Robinson scowled. "What do you think?"

40

"I agree with their assessment. He's getting kicked out of the military so he's gonna lose his Technician job. He's having family problems, they said his high-school daughter's pregnant, and you know, he's probably not very anxious to talk to anybody right now."

"OK. He's got problems. So? We've all got problems." Robinson stepped inside the office and closed the door behind him. "Dimond, you know what I'm asking. Stop sounding like a bleeding-heart crybaby and tell me the truth. Why is he being non-retained?"

"Colonel, I've been up to the Air Guard Base twice. Colonel Hart's talking bullshit about commander's rights and manning needs, and Senior Master Sergeant Cockran isn't talking at all."

"Listen, Super Cooper, you've got to figure this out and come clean with me. Now, you know something or you wouldn't have told me the situation stinks and that somebody's hiding something. Remember how you said somebody was lying? Now, tell me. What do you know?"

"Sir? What do you know? You put me on this case because you got wind of something. Tell me what you suspect and what you're afraid might happen."

Robinson rubbed his bald head. "OK, fair enough. But I can't say much. Seems there might have been some 'unpleasantries' during a drill weekend. That's all I know. Now, tell me. What do you know?"

"I know a terrible incident happened. And I know that Cockran filed a restricted report on it. That means nobody can talk about it. Not even the person he told it to."

"It's true then isn't it." The scowl disappeared from Robinson's face. He almost looked sad. "Cockran was raped."

"How do you know that sir? Who told you that?"

"I can't say. It's just something I heard."

"Colonel, you shouldn't have heard that. Nobody should have heard that. The report Cockran filed was confidential."

"I know all about it. Some woman, a Chief I think. Isn't that what the Air Force calls its E-9s? Chiefs? Anyway, this female Chief took Cockran home from the base club last Saturday night of drill and raped his ass."

"What?"

"Yeah. Used a toy dick I guess. Unless she's one of those hermaphrodite bitches. Never know nowadays."

"Well…fuck."

"Yeah, no shit. So that's what I heard Coop. OK? But I need it confirmed. Got me? I need it O-fish-el!" Robinson looked at his watch and moved toward the door. "Gotta go meet with TAG." He hesitated: "Confirm it, Coop. That's why I put you on this case. We gotta save Cockran from being non-retained."

13.

Dimond Cooper
Friday, 11 March
Memorandum For Record (MFR)

//CLASSIFIED//

MFR #2 for 11 March: Just spoke with COL Robinson, and he informed me that he already knew what happened to SMS Jaxston Cockran. How? I can only deduce that Cockran's situation is an open secret. Everybody in the Air Guard probably knows what happened to him. Or at least, everybody in the Air Guard probably has an idea of what happened to him. Sad.

Looks like a third trip to the Air Guard Base. Now I'm on the hunt for the *woman* who raped Cockran. Woman? Damn. And she's a Chief Master Sergeant? God help us.

Well, at least she'll be easy to find. There can't be more than two or three female Chiefs in the whole state. I'll ask Human Resources to run a manning document and find her name.

So what does this mean? An NCO gets raped and then loses his military position because of it? WTF? I guess I'm back on the road to the Air Guard Base. I'll have Colonel Robinson set-up my meeting with Colonel Hart on Monday morning. This time I'm on OFFICIAL business asking OFFICIAL questions.

The truth? We're about to find out. I hope.

//CLASSIFIED//

14.

"Good morning," the gate guard said. "Can I help you?"

Cooper was definitely ready this time. He clutched his driver's license *and* CAC card like a magician shuffling a deck of cards. He fanned them out for the guard to choose.

"Which card do you need to see?"

The gate guard lifted a hand to his ear. "What say?"

"I said, which card do you need to see?"

"Can I help you with something?"

Cooper smiled. "Don't you remember me? I was here a couple times last week."

"Yeah. I think I do." The guard rested his arm on the car's open window, leaning in and getting comfortable like talking to a friend in the alley. "You here to see the Wing Ding again?"

"Wing Ding? I've never heard the Wing Commander called that before."

"Wing King?"

"Wing Ding," Cooper said.

"He's the Wing Commander."

"Right."

"That would be Colonel Hart. Thought I told you that last week?"

"Yes, you did tell me that last week."

"You sure?" The old guard stood and removed his hat for a quick scratch. "I could swear you were in here last week.

Wanted to see the commander about something? Maybe I've mistaken you for a different young man."

"No, no. I'm the guy."

"Uh-huh. OK then. Have a good day."

Cooper flashed his cards again. "You don't need to see my card?"

"Gets busy here some days," the guard said. "Don't always have time to take it easy and just, you know, shoot the shit. I'm responsible for protecting this base, young man, keeping out the riffraff."

"You're doing a good job, sir."

"Well, 'ppreciate that, but it's no good butterin' me up. I got a job to do. Oughta have your card out and ready so's you don't hold up the line."

"Yes sir. Always be ready."

"That's the way. Slow and steady." The guard shuffled back to the gatehouse. "Have a good day."

"You too!"

A1C Thurston looked up from her cell phone when Cooper opened the glass doors to the Commander's Office, but she didn't stop texting, just pointed to Colonel Hart's open door.

"Go on in?" Cooper asked.

She nodded her head and waved him on.

Cooper knocked on the open door and Colonel Hart spinned from his computer monitor to face him. "Mr. Cooper. Come on in. Have a seat."

"Thank you sir. And by the way, I'm Coop. Been Coop since the first grade. Hope I'm not interrupting?"

"No. Colonel Robinson called and said you were coming. Said you uncovered some mysterious evidence I should know about. He sounded very cryptic on the phone."

"Oh really? Well sir, I don't know if it's all that big a deal, I just wanted Colonel Robinson to call you and set up this appointment to, you know, make it all official-like."

"He did that. And now I'm anxious to hear what you've discovered. Is this about the decision not to reenlist Senior Master Sergeant Cockran?"

"Colonel I like your style. You get right down to business."

"Didn't we just talk about this last week? You were here nosing around and I told you it was, basically, none of your business. Remember?"

"Well, yes. I do remember you telling me that. I also remember somebody else here accusing me of nosing around. One of your Chiefs."

"Is that right?"

"Yes sir. I'm wondering how that Chief even knew why I was here?"

"You know Chiefs, Mr. Cooper."

"Coop. Yes sir, I do know Chiefs. You might have heard, I was a Lieutenant Colonel myself before retiring and putting on this civilian tie."

"I heard that. I also heard you used to work here."

"I retired militarily from here, Colonel. Many moons ago."

"Then you know how effective Chiefs really are. Very resourceful people. Leaders of the NCO force."

"Yes sir. But thinking about it now? I wonder how that Chief knew who I was or why I was here?"

Hart leaned his chair back, removing his eyeglasses and twirling them slowly. "As a retired Lieutenant Colonel, I shouldn't have to tell you twice. You should know that commanders have the power to run their organizations as they see fit."

"Don't have to tell me twice, sir. I understand commanders have a wide latitude. But having wide latitude and breaking the law are different things."

"Is that what you discovered here last week? One of my commanders broke the law?"

"Not exactly."

"What then. Exactly."

"Well, sir, how do I say it? Since you're a man who gets straight to the point, bluntly I guess. What I discovered is, one of your people, don't know if it was a commander or not, but one of your people learned about a restricted report that Senior

47

Master Sergeant Cockran filed, and that person leaked information."

"Leaked?"

"Leaked, spilled, sprayed like a water hose, use the description you like, but he opened his mouth instead of acting like a trusted agent."

"None of my commanders would do that."

"Like I say, don't know if it was a commander."

"Nobody in my chain-of-command would do that. They all know better, especially Lieutenant Colonel Leslie."

"Leslie is Cockran's commander? The guy not allowing Cockran to reenlist?"

"I told you, reenlisting is a military decision, Mr. Cooper. HR on the Technician side has no business looking into how we run our organization, judging us from State HQ like some supreme allied command." Hart's face reddened and he stopped blinking. "You tell Colonel Robinson that I'm about to call The Adjutant General on this!"

Cooper raised his open hands like a shield. "Whoa. Yes sir. I understand. I understand. I'm sure Colonel Robinson is on your side sir."

"He's got a funny way of showing it!"

"Well, you must admit that something's not right here. And Colonel Robinson is just trying to protect TAG's butt on this one. That's all."

Hart slipped his glasses back on. "I just don't understand why this is so hard for you people to understand. Cockran is not a good fit, OK? So Lieutenant Colonel Leslie is forcing him to retire. Simple."

"Yes sir, yes sir. Got that. But, the thing is, sir, this secret that's slipped out? This restricted report that one of your people has leaked? Well, you know, it changes things. What if the media hears about it? Now not allowing Cockran to reenlist puts The Adjutant General's butt on the line. And, you know, that's not cool."

"How's the media going to find out?"

"Cockran could tell them."

"That pussy's afraid of his own shadow. He's not going to go to the media."

"Sir?"

"Look Mr. Cooper. I'm getting tired of this shit. We all know what happened, OK? And I won't stand for that kind of, of, of weakness in my Wing. Especially if all I have to do is keep the guy from reenlisting. He gets to retire, for god sakes. It's not like we're really hurting him."

"Yes sir. It's just that, we don't know what happened, not really. And that's posing problems."

"You've seen Cockran's report?"

"No sir. He filed a restricted report. Except for the EO Officer, nobody should have seen it- not even you. I've just heard rumors. My investigation hasn't uncovered much."

"Your investigation is shit."

"Yes sir."

"You want to know what happened? I'll tell you what happened. Cockran was at the base club faggin' off and he ran into a bull dyke with sharper horns than he had, OK? Now he wants to cry about it and ruin her career? I ain't havin' it."

"The bull dyke wouldn't be Chief Whiteman?"

Hart's glasses magnified his eyes as big as saucers. "OK. So your investigation turned up the only female Chief in the Wing. So? Chief Whiteman is a Traditional Guardsman. Works in AMMO."

"Right- 'If you ain't AMMO you ain't shit.' I've seen that saying scribbled around the base before. AMMO troops used to have it printed on their t-shirts, the ones they wore under their BDU blouse?"

"Yeah, listen Mr. Cooper, this game is getting old. Tell Colonel Robinson to stay in his lane. I'm in charge of this Air Base. I'll make the decisions on who serves here. Got it?"

"Oh yes sir. Got it. I guess that's all then." Cooper stood and turned to leave but hesitated for a second. "Just one more thing, Colonel Hart."

"Yeah?"

"Well, sir, I just wanted to tell you that I really do admire your style. I mean, you're not afraid of taking the heat for the leaked report, and you're not afraid to stand up for your Wing

50

and make a command decision to remove Cockran. The buck stops here, right?"

"Mr. Cooper. Maybe the reason you didn't get promoted to full-bird colonel before you retired is you don't understand what it takes to lead. A commander needs balls. That report never leaked. But, regardless, even if it did leak? I'll take the heat for the good of this Wing."

"Yes sir, I can see that now, you're the man. I'm just a technocrat with bills and a mortgage. I admire your strength." Cooper moved again to leave and said: "Oh yeah, I better tell you about that mysterious evidence. I'm sure you don't really care about it, but Colonel Robinson will ask if I told you."

Hart waited without saying a word.

"So, rumor has it, the phone contains pictures of the assault."

Hart wrinkled his nose and removed his glasses. "What are you talking about?"

"Like I say, I can't read Cockran's report, and the rules say you can't either. But Colonel Robinson wanted me to tell you that Cockran mentioned a cell phone in that report."

"A cell phone?"

"Well, I guess Cockran got a copy of the report, after he filed it, and noticed that the phone had been left out. So he called Colonel Robinson to complain and said he wants to file an addendum to the report to make sure the cell phone gets mentioned. He also wants the phone confiscated for evidence

51

but, of course, that won't happen unless he files formal assault charges."

"Whose phone is it?"

"Don't know. Cockran said the Chief used it to record and take pictures, I guess of the rape. Anyway, the rumor is, you're in a few of those pictures. Probably just a couple shots of you with Cockran at the base club, don't you think? Right before he was assaulted at the hotel? I mean, surely you're not pictured at the hotel. Anyway. Those are just pictures. They don't prove you had anything to do with anything. Kind of bad but you'll manage. You're the man!"

Cooper tried the AGE Shop on a whim. He didn't expect SMS Cockran to be there and, if he was, he didn't expect Cockran to be open to conversation. And he was right on both accounts.

"Hey Mr. Cooper." It was the Technical Sergeant in the coveralls. He was playing euchre at the break table with the other Technicians.

"Coop. Been Coop since first grade."

All four Technicians called in unison: "C-O-O-P!"

"That's more like it. You heroes seen Senior Master Sergeant Cockran?"

"Yep. But he still ain't talkin'. Saw you out the window there, just now when you were crossing the railroad track? He scooted out like a shot deer."

"Who's his supervisor? He can't just take off anytime he wants, can he?"

"Come on, Coop. He's the supervisor."

"Yeah?"

"We just leave him alone. He's going through some hard stuff right now."

"I heard. Did you give him my card and tell him to call me?"

"Yep."

"OK then. I won't interrupt your guys' game. See ya!"

"Hey Coop- were you serious about us being protected by the union here even if we don't pay dues? 'Cause we got a grievance to file."

"Yeah, I'm serious. Get hold of your union president, Mr. Lincoln."

"Chad Lincoln?"

"Yes."

"That moron? He's the union president?"

"Yes. That moron. What's your grievance?"

"Those fuckers took our pop machine!"

"Ooh! That old one that was over there in the corner? I remember seeing it last week. Was gonna buy a pop while I was playing solitaire but the only thing in it was root beer."

"Nah. It was loaded with everything. But it was old and the selection lights didn't work right."

"Who took it out?"

"You know Sergeant Collins? From the Safety Office?"

"No. I don't think so."

"Well, anyway. He said it wasn't safe anymore."

"Was it?"

"Nothin' wrong with that machine. Except for the selection lights."

"Where do you get your pop now?"

"We gotta walk over to the hangar break room. Takes 'bout 10-12 minutes of our break time."

"That's not right."

"Hell no it's not. Cuts in on our euchre time."

"Huh. Well, get hold of ol' Chad."

"Thanks Coop!"

"You bet. Good luck."

15.

Dimond Cooper
Monday, 14 March
Memorandum For Record (MFR)

//FOR OFFICIAL AUTHORIZATION ONLY //

OK, I don't want to confess this. And I especially don't want to confess this in an official memorandum. But, in case of a future investigation, here goes: I might have been less-than-entirely truthful to the Wing Commander.

For The Record: I traveled to the Air Guard Base this morning to interview Col. Hart and get the low-down on why SMS Cockran is being denied reenlistment. Of course, Col. Hart stonewalled me, so I mentioned the cell phone used to record Cockran's assault. What cell phone you ask? The one I made up.

Full disclosure: I told Col. Hart that SMS Cockran wants to add information to his initial report, that he wants to reveal a cell phone used to take pictures of the assault and, oh by the way, those pictures show Col. Hart with Cockran. I also made it seem likely the media might get copies of these non-existent, career-damning pics.

What happens next? Don't know. Col. Hart will probably demand an investigation into my investigation. Guess I'm a terrible bureaucrat.

Change is difficult. We all know this. And change in the military culture might be the hardest of all, what with our myriad of traditions and time-honored ways, all that bullshit. Col. Hart doesn't want to reenlist SMS Cockran because he thinks Cockran is weak. A weak homosexual. And that's the root cause of this issue. Time to change, Col. Hart. Like it or not, weak airman- homos and heteros- have rights.

Anyway, back to my soul searching: Did I lie to the Wing Commander? Is talking about rumored pictures on a cell phone that doesn't exist actually a lie? I'll be completely honest here and say… Maybe, maybe not. At this point I must invoke my 5th Amendment right not to incriminate myself.

Given the chance, would I do the same thing all over again? I must say… Probably.

Am I going to shred this MFR as soon as this issue is settled and no investigation is started? That answer is… Yes!

//FOR OFFICIAL AUTHORIZATION ONLY //

16.

Cooper finished writing the latest MFR and his office telephone rang. "Hello," he said. "This is HR. I'm Coop. How can I help you?"

"Coop! What's up brother?" The voice belonged to Major Newman.

"Doin' fine. Just sittin' in my office enjoying the life of a bureaucrat. You know."

"Yeah, I know, livin' the dream."

"You know that, Newman my man. So what's up?"

"I wanted to talk to you when you were at the base today, but everybody's watching everybody around here. It's like a damned nest of Nazis! Thought it'd just be safer to call you. You alone? Talk a minute?"

"Major Newman I've always got a minute for the legend. Hold on a sec." Cooper put down the phone and stepped over to close his office door. "OK, my man. What's up?"

"You haven't used my name yet, have you?"

"What do you mean, 'yet'?"

"Dude, I know you. Sometimes you let names slip."

"Newman you're hurting my feelings. I mean, I'm absolutely appalled that you would think-"

"OK Coop. OK. Got some more news you might like."

"Yeah?"

"Seriously though, bud, my name is nowhere to be found in your report. OK?"

"You betcha."

"OK. Well, it seems Cockran was raped, get this, by a woman."

Cooper waited. "Yeah?"

"Yeah man. A woman assaulted him."

"That's all you got? Jeez, Newman, here I am waiting for something big. Thought you were gonna tell me the Mona Lisa is a fake or something."

"What?"

"I already know Cockran was raped by a woman."

"Bullshit. Who told you?"

"I can't say."

"Why?"

"It's an investigation, Newman! Besides, I can't just name names. Wouldn't be ethical. You wouldn't like it, would you?"

"You promised me."

"Yeah?"

"Did you promise him?"

"Who?"

"The guy who told you the rapist was a woman."

"Dude. This isn't the third grade."

"Did you promise him?"

"No."

"Then who was it that told you?" Newman's voice ratcheted higher. "Who was it, Coop?"

"I can't say-"

"Coop? Cooooooop? Who was it?"

"I can't come out and say it."

"Was it the Wing Commander?"

"Well, the Wing King knew the assailant was female."

"I knew it!"

"How'd you know?"

"That means Colonel Hart read the restricted report."

"It does?"

"Coop! Think about it. If Hart doesn't read the report, then how does he know it was a female rapist?"

"The EO Officer could've told him."

"No way. That's Captain Barnes."

"I don't know him."

"Barnes is so straight he sleeps standing up. Still young enough to be an idealist. He wouldn't talk."

"What if Colonel Hart threatened him with his job?"

"Barnes is a traditional," Newman said. "Weekends only. He's a dentist, for cryin' out loud. He doesn't need the Guard for money. He wouldn't talk."

"Hmm. So? What difference does it make? I mean, really. What if Colonel Hart did read the report?"

"Coop! It's against the rules for him to read that report. Nobody can read it until Cockran releases it. IF Cockran releases it."

"OK. Yes, I know that. But knowing Hart read it, and proving Hart read it are two separate things."

"That sumbitch broke the rules! Not cool, Coop. Not cool."

"Hey, I agree. But here's the puzzling thing to me, why doesn't Hart go after the attacker? Female or not? Why is he kicking Cockran out of the force?"

"Oh, this is a classic case. It's just turned on its ear. Chicks say it happens all the time."

"They do?"

"Fuckin' eh. You know, they say a dude harasses them and when they complain about it, their boss retaliates against them."

"I guess."

"Same same, Coop, same same. The victim always gets screwed twice."

"I guess. This isn't cool, treating a senior NCO this way."

"It's not cool treating anybody this way."

"You're right."

"Well! Think about it. Does the Wing King want a reporter asking questions about one of his airmen being raped? No! And the rapist is a female? Get the hell outa here!"

"Easier to just kick the victim out."

"You got it!"

Someone knocked on Cooper's door.

"Newman, dude, thanks for the update. Someone's at my door. Gotta go."

"OK. Remember- don't use my name for anything."

"How could I? You didn't tell me shit I don't already know."

"Uh-huh. You're a worthless fraidy-cat sissy with no balls. Did you know that?"

"You say the nicest things."

"OK. I'm out."

"See ya!"

Cooper hung up the phone and opened his door.

"You are in today! I thought I heard your voice Mr. Cooper."

"Coop."

"Oh that's right- Coop. Can I talk to you a minute?"

"Sure. Come on in."

Joy Lovejoy stepped into Cooper's office hips first, like a runway model, a yellow dress hugging her figure and swirling above shiny black high-heels.

"I know I've still got some time to decide on my grievance thing," she said. "It's only been a week or so, but I wanted to talk some more about it."

"Absolutely. Have a seat."

"Have you heard anything from Colonel Lester?"

Cooper shook his head. "Your boss?"

61

"He's acting funny."

"You told me not to say anything so I haven't talked to him."

"Oh I know. But he's acting funny."

"What's he doing?"

"Nothing."

"What do you mean? Is he still eyeballing your, uh, staring at you inappropriately?"

"No! He's looking me right in the eyes like you do. Are you sure you haven't talked to him?"

"Scout's honor. Haven't said a word to Colonel Lester."

"Well, it's just that, you know, I figured you might have said something to warn him because he has just treated me awful since last week."

"How so?"

"He just says, 'Yes, Ms. Lovejoy' and 'No, Ms. Lovejoy.' Always looking me in the eyes and being, well you know, kind of mean."

Cooper reached across his desk and opened a plastic tub of red licorice. He pulled out a rope and offered the container to Lovejoy.

"No thanks," she said.

"Got hooked on these after I quit smoking," Cooper said. "Helps with the stress sometimes."

"Really? When did you quit?"

"February 27."

"Wow. Not too long ago. Think you'll kick the habit?"

"Smoking? Yes. I haven't smoked since February 27, 1993. But eating licorice? I dunno. I've gained 14 pounds but still keep pulling out these red sticks of rehabilitation. I'm like a junky. Pow! Sugar straight to the vein."

"You're funny."

"Thanks. It's the truth though. Tobacco was killing my lungs. Now sugar is killing everything else. Oh well, whatdaya gonna do?"

She laughed that deep, throaty laugh he remembered from last week- the one that clashed with her face.

"Seriously though, ma'am. I did not talk to Colonel Lester about your grievances. But didn't you want him to stop staring at you? Start treating you with respect? I thought that was your whole concern?"

"Well, yeah, but not like this. I mean, I don't want him not to like me anymore, you know? And I don't want him to start treating me like I'm a man."

"Like you're a man?"

"Yeah, you know, 'Ms. Lovejoy, please do this. Ms. Lovejoy, here's your assignment. Ms. Lovejoy, don't do that.' I'm not just some faceless worker bee. I'm a woman too."

"Yes," Cooper said, pulling out another red rope of sugar and dropping his eyes to avoid the temptation of her plunging neckline. "Yes you are."

17.

Dimond Cooper
Monday, 14 March
Memorandum For Record (MFR)

//UNCLASS//

MFR #2 for 14 March: This would be a great place to work if it wasn't for the people. Sheesh. Ms. Joy Lovejoy stopped in to see me today. Seems she's unhappy with COL Lester's changed behavior: He no longer stares at her breasts and now he makes her work. She says it's unacceptable.

I told her she has until next Friday to make up her mind about filing a grievance. After that, the official timeline for grievance filing has closed.

She said, "But what if he goes back to eyeballing me all the time and undressing me with his eyes?"

Wow. Let me be honest with myself (and whoever is reading this MFR) and say: Joy Lovejoy is really well shaped! And I know this is sexist to say, but I can see COL Lester's dilemma. It's all I can do to talk to Ms. Lovejoy and keep looking into her eyes and not let my gaze slip down to her breasts...

Anyway, I told Ms. Lovejoy that if it happens again, then a new grievance timeline starts.

"So every time he looks at my boobies the clock starts again?" (Her words, not mine.)

I can't make this stuff up.

//UNCLASS//

18.

"Coop!" Colonel Robinson yelled from the conference room and his voice washed through the HR office like a wave crashing on the beach. "Coop!"

"Yes sir!" Cooper covered his phone's mouthpiece and shouted back. "Be right there."

Monday morning meeting time again. Cooper on the phone again. Cooper late again. Why did this always happen?

"Coop!"

Another two minutes passed before Dimond Cooper strolled into the already-packed conference room carrying a clipboard and a steaming cup of coffee. The pre-meeting whispering stopped and the attendees stared. Cooper smelled that matchless combination of pity and malice being overwhelmed by apathy.

"Coop, I'm beginning to suspect your faggo- I mean, sissy tie is somehow hindering your ability to discern time."

"Timing wins the battle sir."

"Timing! That's right!" Robinson raised his wrist and tapped his watch for all to see. "My meetings start at 0900."

"Yes sir, I'm fully cognizant of your meetings' mandated start time."

"It's now 0905."

"Thank you sir."

"OK then." Robinson pointed to the meeting's facilitator and said, "Let's go."

"Yes sir. First up today is Spyros with Services' Branch. Anything to cover this week, Spyros?"

Spyros had lots to cover. So did Phil in Benefits. And Marlene in Retirements. Everyone had something to cover.

When Cooper's turn to talk finally rolled around, he almost passed. Then he said: "Sorry I was late Boss. I was on the phone with a Technician from the Air Guard Base. Seems a supervisor up there moved the pop machine out of the building without bargaining with the union."

"You're kiddin'?" Robinson said. "A pop machine can't be moved without asking the union mother-may-I?"

"Sir, it's called I&I bargaining. Impact and Implementation. Moving the pop machine changes a working condition."

Robinson scowled. "So?"

"So, management will have to move the pop machine back."

"What if the commander refuses?"

"The union will file a U.L.P."

"U.L.-"

"Unfair Labor Practice," Cooper said. "It means TAG will be called to federal court to explain why he violated the law."

"Oh no, no, no! That can't happen. You get up to that Air Guard Base, Coop. Explain to those union dipshits that that can't happen."

"Sir, I think the dipshits in this case are called 'management.' They should've offered the union a chance to bargain removal of the pop machine. Now management has to move the pop machine back to exactly where it was, or TAG gets hit with a U.L.P."

"We can't make the commander move that pop machine back," Robinson said. "That'll look like we're siding with those union dipshits."

"Again, sir, I don't think 'dipshits' is the appropriate adjective here."

"Should've said 'union members' instead," SGM Chesterson said.

Robinson cleared his throat. "Right you are, Chet," he said. "Thank you. But I will say management is still in charge of the Air Guard Base up there, that the commander is still the boss. Can't I say that, Coop?"

"Yes sir, you can say that. But the law says the base's management will bargain any changes in working conditions with the union."

"Changes in working conditions?"

"Yes sir."

"OK then. Fair enough. I guess I'm still having a hard time understanding how the union represents the military, but thanks for keeping me straight, Coop."

"Yes sir. It gets confusing. Just remember that Technicians are federal employees during the week. They are not military personnel."

"OK, they're federal employees. But they still wear the uniform?"

"Yes sir, they still wear the uniform because the law says they have to wear the uniform to keep their Technician jobs. The law also says they have the right to be represented by the union."

"I don't like it."

"Yes sir. Noted. You can call your congressman to voice your displeasure with the law. Maybe he'll hop up and make the appropriate changes."

Robinson tilted his head and stared hard at Cooper. "Thanks for that advice."

"Yes sir."

"Anything else?"

"There is one other thing. Can I see you for a minute after this meeting?"

"Is it about Lovej-, uh, that one grievance we've been looking for?"

"Nothing on that, sir. Just wanted to update you on other happenings at the Air Guard Base."

"Other happenings at the Air Guard Base? What? Unauthorized pop machine moves aren't enough?"

Polite laughter sprinkled across the room.

"Sir, it's about that other thing."

"Yeah, OK." Robinson rubbed his bald head. "About that other thing. There's some good news on that, Coop."

"Good news?"

"Yeah. Got a call from Colonel Hart about it this morning. He wants to change the enlistment code on that Senior Master Sergeant, you know, the one at the Air Base causing this issue."

"Sir?"

"Yeah, he said a paperwork error was made. He's got a new administrative assistant up there, you know." Robinson looked around the room and smiled. "See how I said 'administrative assistant' instead of 'secretary'? I'm old, Chet, but I'm learning. I'm learning."

Cooper waited.

"Guess she's a two-striper," Robinson said. "Young and inexperienced. Plays on her smart phone all day."

"Her name is Thurston," Cooper said. "So let me get this straight: Thurston coded our man wrong, so now Colonel Hart will just change the code and let the Senior Master Sergeant reenlist?"

"You make it sound so easy, Coop."

"Sir, it sounds unbelievable to me."

"Well, I don't want to get into the weeds too much here, but Colonel Hart asked about pictures on a cell phone. You know anything about that?"

"I'm not aware of any cell phone pictures."

70

"Hmm. Didn't think so. Anyway, we can talk offline but somehow I think this issue is resolved. The Senior Master Sergeant can reenlist and that will be that. FM. So, good work Coop."

"Unbelievable."

"You're an outstanding bureaucrat with a silver tongue and integrity to spare," Robinson said. "About time you did something to earn your keep."

"Yes sir. Unbelievable."

19.

Dimond Cooper
Monday, 21 March
Memorandum For Record (MFR)

//UNCLASS//

Senior Master Sergeant Jaxston Cockran wins! He is now
being allowed to reenlist into the Air National Guard. Yes!
That means he gets to keep his fulltime Technician job during
the week, i.e., he won't get screwed a second time.

And how did this happen? Why did Colonel Hart change
his mind and let Cockran reenlist?

I like to think the Air Force's Core Values guided Colonel
Hart's decision. There he was, up at the Air Guard Base, in his
office looking out to the flight line, when an epiphany crackled
from On High, and he instantly recognized SMS Cockran's
worth and took righteous actions to thwart a grave injustice
just in the nick of time! (Do you "thwart" an injustice?)
Anyway, that's what I like to think.

The real reason is probably too ugly to look at: Hart
covered his own ass, afraid of the thundering shit storm.

Of course, he boasted of being a real colonel, with the balls
to take the heat and the inner well of strength to do the right
thing no matter the consequences.

What a joker. Where have all the good guys gone?

Anyway, COL Robinson told me in private today that, "We've got to stick together on this thing. Keep our stories straight."

I guess that was his gentlemanly way of saying he knows I lied to Hart about the non-existent cell phone pictures. Robinson said I was an outstanding bureaucrat with a silver tongue. Said he admired my integrity.

Wow. Should I feel vindicated about my lie to Col. Hart? (Yes, OK, I admit it, I lied.) What's that say about my integrity? I mean, John Wayne wouldn't approve, I know this. But my lie did save SMS Cockran's career and prevent an injustice.

I know, a lie is a lie is a lie. But maybe the Scales of Justice are rusty? I mean, if my little white lie balanced a rape, then so be it. I had to be a good Wingman.

FOR THE RECORD: Screw you Col. Hart. You, sir, are a bastard.

//UNCLASS//

20.

"Knock knock." The female voice chimed softly.

Dimond Cooper turned in his chair to see Joy Lovejoy standing in his office doorway.

"Good morning Ms. Lovejoy."

"Hi Coop. Good morning. Thought I better let you know I'm standing here. Not like a couple weeks ago when I made you spill your coffee."

"Uh, right. Come on in."

"Did that coffee ruin your tie? I could try to wash it out for you."

"No, no. It's no problem. Washed right out."

"You didn't have to dry clean it?"

"Actually, my wife took care of it for me," Cooper said. "So I really don't know. Anyway, what can I help you with this morning?"

"I thought you were married." Lovejoy sat down across the desk from Cooper. "You must love your wife, huh?"

"Well...Yes. I do love my wife."

"I'd say, because I never see you looking at other women."

"I try to, you know, I always try to stay professional."

"Oh you do. And there's a difference between being a professional and being a jerk."

"Yes."

Joy Lovejoy wore a purple dress today and it fell modestly below her knees. Glossy white buttons lined the center of the dress, decorating the purple fabric and restraining the pressure of her bulging breasts. She sat prim and proper, with a sweet smile, and seemed in no hurry to say anything.

Cooper said: "Are you here to finally file that grievance?"

"No," Lovejoy said. "I've decided to just let it be. It's like I say, there's a difference between being a professional and being a jerk."

"Yes. So which one is Colonel Lester? Professional or jerk?"

"Well, that's why I came in here to see you last week, or the week before last, whenever it was."

"Yes?"

"I thought then that he was being a jerk."

"And now?"

"Now I know he wasn't. He's a professional, but he's just not as professional as some people, like you."

"What do you mean?"

"He can't help looking at my boobies."

"Listen, we can force him to get some training and-"

"Oh no, really, I don't think he can help it. And, you know, after I thought about it a little bit, I was like, you know, I really shouldn't be mad at him. He's never touched me or said anything, you know, anything-"

"Inappropriate?"

"Right. He never has. He just can't keep from looking at them."

"Well, that's gotta make you feel uncomfortable though."

"Not really, Coop. My boobies got big early, I mean, like when I was 12-years-old? I was already wearing my mom's C-cup. And everybody looks, even women. So, why should he be different?"

"OK, but what happened to make you think about filing a grievance to begin with? I mean, if all he did was look, and looking doesn't necessarily offend you..."

"Maybe I was mad about something. Something else. Whatever. You know I wasn't thinking straight. Maybe I felt sorry for myself or something. Anyway, I've been blessed with a big chest. And, you know, that shouldn't disrupt Colonel Lester's career."

"Well, then, for the record, you are not filing a grievance against Colonel Lester?"

"No, I am not."

"And you're not going to file an EO complaint against him for looking at your, for looking at you inappropriately?"

"No."

"OK, good, then. It's officially settled."

Joy Lovejoy smiled and pointed a finger at Cooper.

"You almost looked," she said.

"What?"

"I saw your eyes. You almost looked."

76

Cooper smiled back and stared deep into Lovejoy's eyes.

She laughed throaty and deep. "You really do love your wife!"

21.

Dimond Cooper
Tuesday, 22 March
"Joy Lovejoy" Final Memorandum For Record

//UNCLASS//

This MFR concerns the disposition of the Joy Lovejoy affair. So, I guess you- whoever you are and whatever agency you work for- won't be reading about the case of Joy Lovejoy anytime soon. I'm going to type up this MFR, put it neatly on top of the pile of "Lovejoy MFRs" and stuff the whole stack into a manila folder in H.R.'s filing cabinet. I'll file it under 'B' for two obvious reasons.

So here goes the wrap-up, Bottom Line Up Front (that's what we in the military bidness call the "BLUF")- Today Ms. Joy Lovejoy officially rejected her opportunity to file a grievance for harassment in the workplace.

FOR THE RECORD: Joy Lovejoy stopped by my office this morning and said she will **not** file a grievance, or an EO complaint, against Colonel Roy Lester.

And, continuing in the parlance of the military, that's that.
//UNCLASS//

22.

"Coop!"

Colonel Jerome Robinson sounded angry. His call for Cooper rang through HR like a fire alarm.

"Coop!"

Cooper was on the phone, explaining to a Technician how the discipline process works. He barely had time to get the Technician's phone number and promise to call back before Robinson invaded his doorway.

"Coop! Didn't you hear me calling for you?"

"Yes sir. I was on the phone."

"Lovejoy? Is she gonna file a grievance or not? She can't keep stringing us along like a prom date!"

"No sir, that wasn't Lovejoy. But she did come in to see me this morning. Officially, she isn't going to file."

"Grievance or EO complaint?"

"Neither. She wants bygones to be bygones."

"Huh." Robinson slumped against the doorframe and rubbed his bald head. "How about that? I thought the good Colonel Lester had pushed too far this time. He must be losing his touch. He's turned into an old man and doesn't threaten the ladies anymore."

"Yes sir. Maybe. Or maybe Joy Lovejoy is a caring person."

Robinson smiled and lowered his head. "Have you looked at her tits? My gawd, man!"

"Yes sir," Cooper said. "Confirms your belief in a higher power."

Both men stood silent for a moment.

"Did you need something Boss?"

Robinson came back from his dream. "Hell yes! What is this shit, Coop? I thought you talked to those dipshits at the Air Guard Base?"

Robinson handed over a letter with a union logo printed at the top. It read:

MEMO: The Adjutant General (TAG)

SUBJECT: Unfair Labor Practice (U.L.P.)

The Union recognized by the Federal Labor Relations Authority (FLRA) to represent federal Technicians at the Air Guard Base is officially informing you of our intention to file an Unfair Labor Practice charge for failure to inform us of a change in working conditions. IAW Section 7106(b) of Public Law 95-454, removal of a pop machine without offering the opportunity to I&I bargain the removal...

Robinson began talking before Cooper could finish reading the letter. "Well?" he said.

"This is a big deal," Cooper said. "TAG seen it?"

"Yeah, he got it yesterday. Wasn't happy. Called his personal lawyer on the phone about it."

"Personal lawyer? What about Colonel Balinski, the JAG? He's paid by the government to work TAG's legal issues."

"TAG's mad at Ski. Called him out in front of everybody in the room."

"Ooh. Not good."

"No, it wasn't." Robinson sighed. "And now he wants answers from me."

"You mean, he wants to know how this happened?"

"Yeah."

"Sir, I told you in this week's meeting that management at the Air Guard Base was putting TAG in the firing line for a U.L.P."

"You did? Yeah, I guess you did, but I didn't understand what you were talking about. I hate this Labor shit. How can the union file a charge against TAG? He didn't even know management at the Air Guard Base moved that pop machine."

Cooper shook his head. "Colonel, all Unfair Labor Practice charges go against the head of the agency. And TAG is the head of this state's National Guard."

"Even if he didn't know what happened?"

"Even if he didn't know."

"That's a bad system. So, now what?"

"Now it's time to engage the union with our hat in our hand. We screwed up."

"I don't like that."

"No sir. Not good."

"Can you make it go away?"

"I am SuperLaborDude. I can try."

Robinson forced a chuckle. "OK Coop. Head back up to the Air Guard Base tomorrow. I'll tell TAG we got our best man on the case. Try to make this go away."

"Yes sir."

"Damn," Robinson said. He rubbed his bald head. "I hate those dipshits."

23.

Dimond Cooper
Tuesday, 22 March
Memorandum For Record (MFR)

//UNCLASS//

MFR #2 for 22 March: The purpose of today's second MFR is CYA, Cover Your Ass, plain and simple. This memo answers any question as to why I'm going to the Air Guard Base tomorrow. So, if anyone develops a bad case of the ass, here's why: COL Robinson is sending me to the Air Base on official business to negotiate a resolution to the U.L.P. filed by the union.

I wonder what that crazy old gate guard will want to see this time? Looks like he struggles a little with PTSD, but he makes the visit worth the price of admission.

Anyway, we'll see what happens. And who said the life of a bureaucrat is boring? This agency represents the best of America- Anything can happen!

Seriously. I can't make this stuff up.

//UNCLASS//